MEERKATS

FLAMINGOS

CITY ZOO

ZOO PHOTOS

ZOO GIFT SHOP

Welcome!
ZOO MAP
WHICH ANIMAL IS YOUR FAVORITE?

"1...2...3...4...5...6...
7...8...9...and Pinky."

Pinky Got Out!

By Michael Portis

Illustrated by Lori Richmond

Crown Books for Young Readers
New York

Home of
PINKY THE
FLAMINGO

"Welcome to the zoo. Showing you around is my favorite thing to do," said the zookeeper. "These birds always stick together. So today, be like a flamingo and stay with your flock."

"Uh-oh," said Penny.

"Next are the meerkats," explained the zookeeper.
"Some forage for food while the scouts watch out for trouble."

"Pinky got out," said Penny.

"Some seals hold their breath while sleeping underwater," said the zookeeper.

"Look..."

"Pinky got out!" said Penny.

"Have you seen Pinky?" asked Penny.

"Who?" asked Mia.

"Pinky!" said Penny.

"The python can grow as long as a garden hose,"
said the zookeeper.

"Pinky!" said Joey.

"He got out," said Penny.

"There's Pinky!" said Penny and Max.

"Don't be silly," said the zookeeper. "This is for giraffes only."

"What happened
to Pinky?" asked Ike.

"We lost him,"
said Penny.

"It's a myth that ostriches stick their heads in the sand to hide," said the zookeeper. "Sometimes it looks that way when they're finding food."

"Pinky got out," said Penny.

"We're coming to the zoo shop, which is the end of our tour," said the zookeeper. "Remember, a flock always stays together."

"Does anyone want to say what they learned today?" asked the zookeeper.

Pinky Got

"Bye-bye, Pinky," said Penny.

Squawk.

"1 . . . 2 . . . 3 . . . 4 . . . 5 . . . 6 . . . 7 . . . 8 . . . 9 . . . and . . . wait," said the zookeeper. "Where's Pinky?"

For Barbara Bottner —M.P.

For Dana, in honor of
sisterly shenanigans —L.R.

Text copyright © 2019 by Michael Portis

Jacket art and interior illustrations copyright © 2019 by Lori Richmond

All rights reserved. Published in the United States by Crown Books for Young Readers,

an imprint of Random House Children's Books, a division of Penguin Random House LLC, New York.

Crown and the colophon are registered trademarks of Penguin Random House LLC.

Visit us on the Web! rhcbooks.com

Educators and librarians, for a variety of teaching tools, visit us at RHTeachersLibrarians.com

Library of Congress Cataloging-in-Publication Data

Names: Portis, Michael. | Richmond, Lori, illustrator.

Title: Pinky got out! / Michael Portis; illustrated by Lori Richmond.

Description: First edition. | New York: Crown Books for Young Readers, [2019] | Summary: When Pinky the flamingo slips out to join

a zoo tour, the children all notice but the zookeeper fails to see Pinky trying to blend in with seals, meerkats, and pandas.

Identifiers: LCCN 2018050336 | ISBN 978-1-101-93298-8 (hardback) | ISBN 978-1-101-93300-8 (epub) | ISBN 978-1-101-93299-5 (glb)

Subjects: | CYAC: Flamingos—Fiction. | Zoos—Fiction. | Zoo animals—Fiction. | Humorous stories. | BISAC: JUVENILE FICTION / Animals

/ Zoos. | JUVENILE FICTION / Animals / Birds. | JUVENILE FICTION / Humorous Stories.

Classification: LCC PZ7.1.P6474 Pin 2019 | DDC [E]—dc23

MANUFACTURED IN CHINA

10 9 8 7 6 5 4 3 2 1   First Edition